About the Book

Odd Jobs was willing to take on any job. The odder the better—that was his motto. So when Dolly Finch needed someone to wash her dog Bouncer, whom did she go to? Odd Jobs, of course. And when Lumpy Edwards needed someone to take his place at dancing class, whom did he turn to? Why, Odd Jobs, naturally. And when Benny Benson needed a balloon sitter to protect his new balloon from his balloon-popping brother, who was his natural choice? Odd Jobs, that's who.

In this easy-to-read storybook Tony Johnston and Tomie de Paola join forces to create a zany character whose comic adventures will brighten the dreariest of days!

THE DOG WASH

story by Tony Johnston
pictures by Tomie de Paola

ODD JOBS
THE
ODDER,
THE
BETTER

A See and Read Storybook

Published by
FIREFLY PAPERBACKS
A Scholastic Book Service

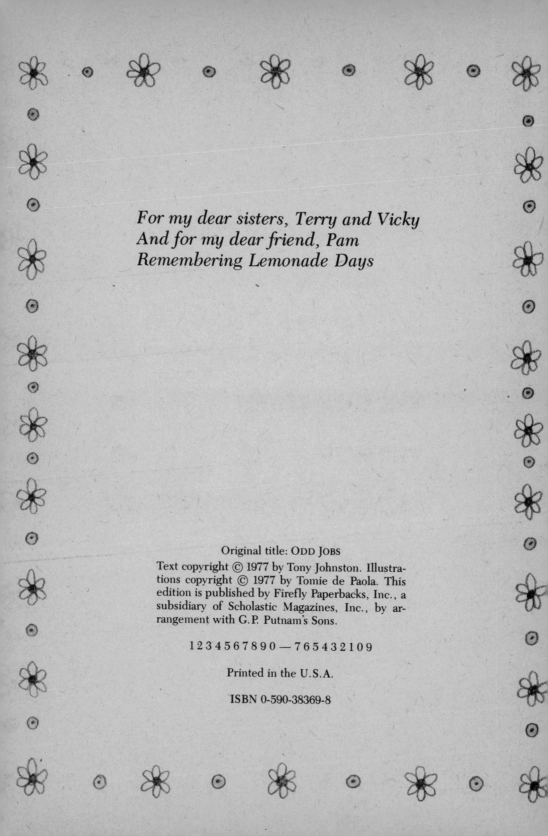

For my dear sisters, Terry and Vicky
And for my dear friend, Pam
Remembering Lemonade Days

Original title: ODD JOBS

Text copyright © 1977 by Tony Johnston. Illustrations copyright © 1977 by Tomie de Paola. This edition is published by Firefly Paperbacks, Inc., a subsidiary of Scholastic Magazines, Inc., by arrangement with G. P. Putnam's Sons.

1 2 3 4 5 6 7 8 9 0 — 7 6 5 4 3 2 1 0 9

Printed in the U.S.A.

ISBN 0-590-38369-8

CONTENTS

THE DOG WASH

"My dog, Bouncer, needs a bath,"
said Dolly Finch.
"Can you do the job?"
"Sure," said Odd Jobs. "For fifty cents."
He did all sorts of jobs. The odder
the better. That was his motto.
"Shake on it," said Dolly Finch.

7

Then Bouncer came out.
Odd Jobs was sorry he shook.

Odd Jobs went home and went to work.
He filled the sink and called Bouncer.
Bouncer came and drank all the water.

Odd Jobs got the hose. Bouncer took it,
shook it, and chewed it up.

"Grrrrr," said Odd Jobs.
He filled a tub and floated a
dog biscuit in the middle. PLOP!
Bouncer jumped in and sat on the dog biscuit.

So Odd Jobs washed him fast.
Bouncer bounced out of the tub
and stood very still. Then . . .
he shook all over and
rolled in the dirt.

Bouncer went back in the tub.
Odd Jobs scrubbed him squeaky clean.
"All right," he said. "Now *stay* clean."

11

So Bouncer jumped over him,
skated across the garage,
galloped into the garden,
and dug up the flowers.

Odd Jobs held out a juicy bone.
"Here, boy," he called.
Bouncer grabbed the bone,

Odd Jobs grabbed Bouncer, and they dashed through the clothesline.

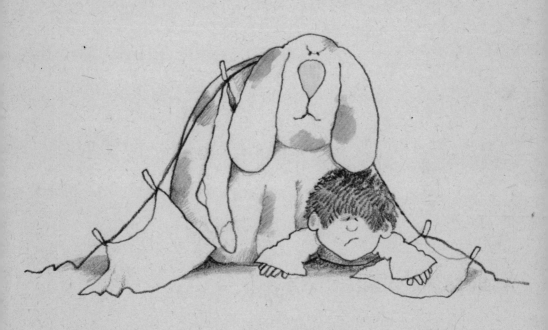

When Bouncer was tired, he sat down. He sat down on top of Odd Jobs.

Bouncer went back in the tub.
Odd Jobs scrubbed him shiny clean.
"Now you sit, and you *stay*," he said.
"I'll get the wagon and take you home."
But Bouncer saw a cat and chased it up a tree.
And he was dirty again.

Odd Jobs sneaked up behind him
with the tub.
"Come!" he called.
SPLOP! Bouncer came so fast
he knocked Odd Jobs into the tub,
jumped in, and gave him a big, muddy hug.

"I love you, too," said Odd Jobs.
"This time you'll stay clean if
I have to *carry* you home."

When the bath was over, Odd Jobs
called his friend Danny.
"Hi, Danny. What are you doing?"
"Nothing."
"Good. Help me carry a dog home."
"OK," said Danny.
They wrapped Bouncer in a beach towel
and carried him home.

Then Bouncer started chewing on the towel.
"Stop that," said Odd Jobs.

He stopped that and started
chewing on Odd Jobs.

So they stopped carrying him—oooph.

And, sure enough, Bouncer was dirty again.
"Dirty or not, you're going home."

"Hi, Dolly," puffed Odd Jobs.
"Here's Bouncer. Can we sit down?"
Dolly Finch looked at Bouncer and said,
"*Gosh!*"
"Did you ever see anything like that?"
asked Odd Jobs proudly.
"No. He's the dirtiest dog I ever saw."
"Well," said Odd Jobs. "Under all that
dirt is the cleanest dog you ever saw.
I bathed him *four times* today."

"Gosh! Four dog washes for fifty cents!"
said Dolly Finch. "But why so many?"
"All part of the job," grumbled Odd Jobs.

THE HOP

One day a voice came from the bushes.
"PSSST, Odd Jobs. PSSST. Come here."
"PSSST, yourself," said Odd Jobs.
"Who is it?"
"Lumpy Edwards," said the voice.
"What's up, Lumpy?"

"I've got a job for you," he began.
"Miss Gollotz has a dancing class,
and I'm in it."
"That's serious," said Odd Jobs.
"What's the job?"
"Take my place."
Odd Jobs said, "No job too big. No job
too small. That's my motto. What's the pay?"
"An all-day sucker. Raspberry."

Odd Jobs went to the dancing class,
wearing his only suit and his favorite hat.
The dancing class had started.
When Odd Jobs came in, it stopped.
Everybody came to read his hat. Miss Gollotz
came to see who was stopping her class.
"Who are you?" she asked.
"Odd Jobs. I'm taking
Lumpy Edwards' place. He couldn't come."
"Well, take off your hat and join the others,"
Miss Gollotz told him.

The dancing class started again.
Then it stopped.
Miss Gollotz collected all the gum.
She collected all the rubber bands.
And the slingshots. And marbles.

The dancing class started again.
"Today we will learn the fox trot,"
said Miss Gollotz.
"I can do the *plain* trot," somebody said.

He trotted around the room, grinning.
"I can gallop," said somebody else. Soon
everybody was trotting and galloping around.
"Whoa!" called Miss Gollotz.

Boys' choice. Odd Jobs had to choose somebody.
He chose Fluffy Murphy. She was tall.
I won't have to talk to her, he thought.
She will be too high up.

Odd Jobs was right. She talked to *him*
the whole time—right over his head.
She chattered about her collection of
four-leaf clovers.
"It's a small collection. They're hard
to find. I mean. You hardly ever find them.
Especially in the city."
"How many do you have?" asked Odd Jobs.
"One."
"That's a small collection, all right."

Girls' choice.

"May I have this dance?" giggled
Fluffy Murphy. Odd Jobs scrunched low.
Maybe she was asking the person next to him.
There wasn't a person next to him. So
he did the bunny hop with Fluffy Murphy.

Side, side. Side, side. Up. Back.
Hop, hop, hop. Side, side. Side, side.
Up. Back. Hop, hop, hop.
Fluffy Murphy chattered the whole time.
Odd Jobs thought about the all-day
sucker the whole time.
He felt like an all-day sucker.

Then he saw an open door.
He hopped with all his might.
"Be-ooo-ti-ful," said Miss Gollotz,
closing her eyes to hear the music.
Hop, hop, hop. The whole class
giggled and hopped
behind Odd Jobs. Down the staircase,
past the coats, and out into
the sunshine.

Lumpy Edwards was waiting alone.

Hop, hop, hop.

He wasn't alone for long.

"How was it?" he asked.

"Great," said Odd Jobs. "We got away."

"Oh, no," groaned Lumpy Edwards.

"Well, here's your all-day sucker."
"Thanks, Lumpy. Will you tell Miss Gollotz
good-bye for me?
"Sure," said Lumpy Edwards. "I like
to bring people good news."

THE BALLOON SITTER

Whenever Benny Benson got new shoes,
he got a new balloon. And his little brother,
Pee Wee, popped it.
Benny had new shoes and a new balloon.
Pee Wee bet him that it wouldn't
last the night. Benny took the bet
and called Odd Jobs.

"Odd Jobs," he said, "I need a
balloon sitter tonight."
"That's for me," said Odd Jobs.
He liked night jobs.
Night jobs are always even dollar jobs.

He took his sleeping bag, his toothbrush,
and his pajamas. And he went to spend
the night with Benny's balloon.

The balloon was blue with black
stenciled letters. It looked tough.
Pee Wee Benson looked tougher.

At dinner Odd Jobs held the balloon,
ate spaghetti, and watched Pee Wee.
"Please pass the butter," said Mrs. Benson.
"Sorry, I can't," said Odd Jobs.
"I have one hand full of spaghetti,
one hand full of balloon, and . . .
hey, where's Pee Wee?"
"He was just here," said Benny.
"Well, he's not here now."

Then Odd Jobs saw Pee Wee Benson
sneaking across the floor with a pin.
"SHOOO!" shouted Odd Jobs.
Pee Wee Benson shooed!

Odd Jobs was brushing his teeth.
He heard a rustle, rustle, rustle.
He saw a peashooter poke out from
the shower curtain.
"GET LOST!" shouted Odd Jobs.
Pee Wee Benson got lost!

Mr. Benson read a story.
But Odd Jobs didn't listen.
He watched Pee Wee Benson, creeping up
with a rubber arrow aimed at the balloon.
"SCRAM!" yelled Odd Jobs.
Pee Wee Benson scrammed!

Odd Jobs scrunched down into his sleeping bag.
He used the balloon for a pillow.
He thought he heard somebody lurking nearby.
So he put the balloon
inside the sleeping bag.

Then he began to worry. What if Pee Wee
tried another pin? What if Pee Wee
popped him?
Odd Jobs took out the balloon and
drew a funny face on it.
He put his hat on it, gave it a pat,
and put it in the chair.
There, he thought. *That will fool Pee Wee.*
"Ho-hum," he yawned and lay down.

"AH-HA!" Pee Wee Benson yelled
and jumped up.
He grabbed for the balloon.
But Odd Jobs got it first.
He held it high over his head.
Pee Wee Benson grinned and
tickled Odd Jobs all over.
Odd Jobs laughed so hard
he let go of the balloon.
And it floated right out the window!

They watched it go up and up.
Suddenly Odd Jobs shouted, "Hey, look!"
The string caught on a branch of a
big tree. The balloon was stuck.

The next morning Benny Benson
saw his balloon in the tree.
"What's my balloon doing up there?" he asked.
"Staying safe from Pee Wee," said Odd Jobs.
"It's a great place for balloons."
"It's a great place for birds," grumbled Benny.
But he paid Odd Jobs the dollar.

Then he said, "See the balloon in that big tree?"
"Yes," said Odd Jobs.
"Well, I need somebody to get it down.
Will you take the job?"
"Not now," said Odd Jobs.
"Now I'm taking a vacation."

About the Author

Tony Johnston grew up in California and attended the University of California at Berkeley and Stanford University, where she got a master's degree in education. She taught elementary school and worked in publishing before moving to Mexico City with her husband. They have two little girls, Jennifer and Samantha. Ms. Johnston is the author of *The Adventures of Mole and Troll, Mole and Troll Trim the Tree* and *The Fig Tale*.

About the Artist

Tomie de Paola was born in Meriden, Connecticut. He received his Bachelor of Arts from the Pratt Institute and his Master of Fine Arts from the California College of Arts and Crafts.

Mr. de Paola has written and/or illustrated over twenty books, many of which have received the highest acclaim in the field of children's books. *Strega Nona*, which he both wrote and illustrated, is a Caldecott Honor Book. He is also a professor in the Visual Arts Department of New England College in Henniker, New Hampshire.